CUTE AND UNUSUAL PETS

HEDGEHOGS

by Paula Wilson

Consultant
Sarrah Kaye
Veterinarian and General Curator
Staten Island Zoo
Staten Island, New York

CAPSTONE PRESS
a capstone imprint

Snap Books are published by Capstone Press,
1710 Roe Crest Drive, North Mankato, Minnesota 56003
www.mycapstone.com

Library of Congress Cataloging-in-Publication Data
Names: Wilson, Paula M., 1963- author.
Title: Hedgehogs / by Paul Wilson.
Description: North Mankato, Minnesota : an imprint of Capstone Press, [2019] | Series: Snap books. Cute and unusual pets | Audience: Age 8-14.
Identifiers: LCCN 2018016113 (print) | LCCN 2018017757 (ebook) | ISBN 9781543530650 (eBook PDF) | ISBN 9781543530568 (hardcover)
Subjects: LCSH: Hedgehogs—Juvenile literature.
Classification: LCC SF459.H43 (ebook) | LCC SF459.H43 W55 2019 (print) | DDC 636.933/2—dc23

Editorial Credits
Lauren Dupuis-Perez, editor
Sara Radka, designer
Kathy McColley, production specialist

Image Credits
Getty Images: Adriana Varela Photography, 14, EyeEm/Che Wei Chooi, 19, EyeEm/Mark Joseph Gatus, 28, GlobalP, 1, luamduan, 4, martinedoucet, 22, pandpstock001, 26, praisaeng, 5; Shutterstock: Elijus3000, 11, Eric Isselee, 29, Jen Huls, 21, kamnuan, 7, Lokicon, cover, Lyudmyla Nikolenko, 25, rzeszutko, 27, Sonsedska Yuliia, back cover, 8, 17, takkaaa, 13, Thanapol thanalad, 20, TrishaFrenchPhotography, 6

Glossary terms are bolded on first use in text.

Printed and bound in the United States of America.
PA65

TABLE OF CONTENTS

CHAPTER 1

MEET THE HEDGEHOG

If you are looking for a pet that is friendly, quiet, and cute, a hedgehog might be for you. Although they are shy animals, hedgehogs bond with their owners. They are also easy to care for and do not need a lot of space. What's another reason hedgehogs are so popular? They do not have bad odors like some pets! Hedgehogs can also be curious and playful. Many hedgehogs cuddle with their caretakers. Even though hedgehogs are not always social, they can be fun and engaging pets.

WHAT'S A HEDGEHOG?

Hedgehogs are **mammals**. They get their name from their behavior in the wild. They hunt and sniff for food underneath hedges and brush. While they are hunting, they make snorting sounds like a pig.

mammal—a warm-blooded animal that breathes air; mammals have hair or fur; female mammals feed milk to their young

DID YOU KNOW?

Hedgehogs are not actually hogs. They are closely related to other small spiny mammals called gymnures and moonrats. They are not related to porcupines, even though they both have pointy spines.

HEDGEHOGS IN THE WILD

Hedgehogs are not **native** to North America. In the wild hedgehogs live in Europe, Asia, and Africa. Hedgehogs are **nocturnal**. They sleep during the day and look for food at night. Some **species** of hedgehogs hibernate in the winter.

Wild hedgehogs help gardens grow by snacking on bugs that often eat plants.

Hedgehogs are **omnivores**. They eat bugs, plants, worms, rodents, lizards, and even snakes. Their eyesight is very poor, but they have a strong sense of smell. Their snouts can sniff out bugs 2 inches (5 centimeters) below ground.

There are 17 hedgehog species. They come in different sizes and colors, and they all behave in different ways. Pet hedgehogs are African pygmies. They are a mix of the white-bellied and Algerian hedgehog species.

SNAKE BITE? NO PROBLEM

Hedgehogs have some protection against snake and insect bites. A protein in their muscles makes them able to withstand snake and insect venom.

native—growing or living naturally in a particular place
nocturnal—active at night and resting during the day
species—a group of animals with common features
omnivore—an animal that eats both plants and other animals

SPIKED HAIR

The hedgehog's spines are actually a type of hair. When a hedgehog is about 6 to 8 weeks old, it loses its baby spines in a process called "quilling." This makes room for its adult spines. The adult spines are all the same length and do not come out. In addition to protection, the spines are used for cushioning if a hedgehog falls. Spines also help keep the animal dry.

SPINES, SNOUTS, AND SQUEALS

What do you notice first about a hedgehog? It's probably the sharp spines that cover its back and sides. These stiff, nonvenomous spines keep the animal safe from **predators**. When frightened, a hedgehog curls into a tight ball. Its spines point outward, protecting it from danger.

---

predator—an animal that hunts other animals for food

The hedgehog's underbelly is covered in white or tan fur. Most hedgehogs have white or cream-colored spines with bands of brown or black. Some hedgehogs have raccoon-like markings on their faces with dark fur around their noses and eyes. Hedgehogs have five toes on their front feet and four toes on their back feet. Their long, pointed noses twitch when they sniff around and explore.

African pygmies are 6 to 8 inches (15 to 20 cm) long. They weigh 18 to 25 ounces (510 to 709 grams). That is about the same weight as two cans of soup. Other species of hedgehog are larger. They can grow to 10.5 inches (27 cm) long and weigh up to 2.25 pounds (1 kilogram). In the wild hedgehogs live for 2 to 3 years.

Hedgehogs make lots of different noises. They communicate with snorts, squeals, puffs, and hisses. Hedgehogs make a clicking sound when they are angry.

DID YOU KNOW?

African pygmies do not hibernate in the winter.

HEDGEHOGS AND HUMANS

People have a long history with hedgehogs. Hedgehogs first appeared in artwork thousands of years ago. Ancient Egyptians showed hedgehogs on ceramic bowls, jewelry, and ships. In the 1500s Shakespeare wrote about hedgehogs in a few of his plays. He called them "hedge-pigs."

Despite the hedgehog's long place in history, they are somewhat new as pets. People first brought hedgehogs to the United States from Africa in the 1970s. Today hedgehogs are popular pets around the world, especially in the United States and the United Kingdom.

HEDGEHOGS HIT HOLLYWOOD

Hedgehogs have captured the imagination of authors, video game creators, and movie makers. Sonic the Hedgehog is a famous video game character. This blue hedgehog with supersonic speed has a huge following. Sonic even has 5 million followers on Twitter! Hedgehogs have also made it to Hollywood. Mr. Pricklepants is a charming hedgehog who appears in the movie *Toy Story 3*.

Clubs, shows, and websites are dedicated to hedgehogs. A convention called Hedgie-Con is held every year in the United States. Social media has helped the hedgehog gain fame and popularity. Facebook and Instagram pages feature life with pet hedgehogs. A hedgehog named Mr. Pokee has 435,000 followers on Instagram and nearly 40,000 followers on Facebook.

Hedgehogs are sometimes called "pogs" or "hedgies."

CHAPTER 2

HEDGEHOGS AS PETS

Caring for a pet is a big responsibility. Although hedgehogs are easier to take care of than many other pets, they still need daily attention. Talk to your parents about owning a hedgehog. Ask yourself these questions before you decide if a hedgehog is right for you:

- Do you have the time to care for a hedgehog? Will you have time to feed it, clean its cage, and play with it?
- How much does a hedgehog cost to buy? How much does its food and other supplies cost? Who will pay for the animal and everything it needs? You or your parents?
- Who will take care of the hedgehog? You or your parents or siblings? Or will you all share in the responsibility?
- Is there a vet in your area who takes care of hedgehogs?
- Do you have space in your home for the hedgehog's cage?

Even though hedgehogs can be independent pets, they still need daily attention.

Due to a hedgehog's small size, it needs to be protected from other pets in the house.

MORE TO KNOW

Do you think you are ready for a pet hedgehog? You'll need to consider a few other things before you get one. Do you have other pets in your home? Cats will usually leave a pet hedgehog alone when they see its sharp spines. However, use caution if introducing dogs to a new hedgehog. Dogs may be aggressive. They could easily harm the hedgehog. Never leave your hedgehog unsupervised in the same room with your cat or dog. If you have other pets, such as rats, lizards, or rabbits, ask a parent to help you research how they get along with hedgehogs.

Before you adopt a hedgehog, make sure the pet is allowed where you live. California, Georgia, Hawaii, Pennsylvania, and New York City have laws against owning hedgehogs. The laws are in place to prevent owners from releasing unwanted hedgehogs into the wild. Freed hedgehogs compete with native animals for food and living space. Also, pet hedgehogs do not have the skills to survive in the wild. If you get a pet hedgehog and then decide that it's not the right pet for you, do not let it go free outside. Find a home for the hedgehog, such as with a **breeder** or with someone who wants to adopt it.

DID YOU KNOW?

It is not necessary to buy more than one hedgehog. They are **solitary** animals that do not need to be with other hedgehogs.

---

breeder—a person who raises animals to sell
solitary—living and hunting alone

CHOOSING YOUR HEDGEHOG

You've decided that a hedgehog is the right pet for you. Now where do you get one? How do you decide which one to get? The best way is from a breeder. He or she will help you choose a hedgehog and show you how to take care of it. There are dozens of breeders across the United States, Canada, and Europe. Another option is to find a rescue agency in your area that has hedgehogs to adopt.

Choose a hedgehog that is healthy and has a good **temperament**. It should have clear and bright eyes, a moist and clean nose, and fur on its underbelly that is not matted. The best time to bring a hedgehog home is when it is 6 to 11 weeks old. At this age the hedgehog can easily **adapt** to its new home and surroundings.

DID YOU KNOW?

Pet hedgehogs cost from $75 to $150. Those with facial markings or rare colors, like white, can cost up to $250.

HANDS OFF!

If you come across a hedgehog in the wild, do not try to take it home as a pet. Hedgehogs in the wild might have diseases that can be passed on to humans. The animal may not be used to human contact and could be aggressive.

VISITING THE VET

Soon after you get your hedgehog, make an appointment with a vet who knows how to take care of the animal. The vet will make sure your pet is healthy. The vet can also give you advice on caring for your new hedgehog. Visit the vet once a year to check your hedgehog's weight and overall health. If your hedgehog ever gets sick, you will have a vet who already knows you and your pet.

---

temperament—the combination of an animal's behavior and personality; the way an animal usually acts or responds to situations shows its temperament

adapt—to change to fit into a new or different situation

CHAPTER 3

CARING FOR YOUR HEDGEHOG

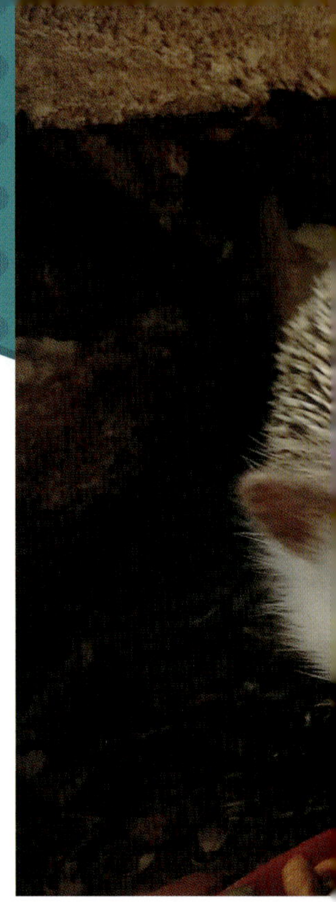

What kind of cage should you get for your hedgehog? What should you feed it? Can you play with it? You may have a lot of questions about how to take care of your hedgehog. Make sure to learn everything you can before you bring your hedgehog home.

HOME, SWEET HEDGEHOG HOME

Hedgehogs need the right cage in order to stay safe and comfortable. They do best in a large cage with a flat bottom, similar to a guinea pig or rabbit cage. These cages are usually 2 feet (61 cm) by 4 feet (122 cm). Cover the bottom with soft bedding. Most pet stores sell bedding made from recycled paper or fluffy pulp. Make sure your hedgehog has plenty of water. Put the water in a bowl or a water bottle attached to the cage. Hedgehogs like to burrow and be covered, especially when they sleep. A miniature sleeping bag is a cozy spot for your hedgehog.

Refill your hedgehog's water container every day.

Hedgehogs can be trained to use a litter box. Put a small box in their cage and fill it with litter pellets. Empty the litter box and clean the animal's food bowls every day. The bedding should be changed and the cage thoroughly cleaned once a week.

It is important to keep your hedgehog warm. Its **environment** should be 72 to 80 degrees Fahrenheit (22 to 27 degrees Celsius). Some breeders suggest using a heating pad under part of the cage or a heat lamp. If African pygmies get too cold, they could go into hibernation. This can be life threatening to them.

---

environment—the surroundings in which a person, animal, or plant lives

MEALS AND FOOD

Pet hedgehogs do well with a diet of dry or canned cat food, along with mealworms, crickets, and chopped vegetables. Dry cat food also works well because it is high in protein. Feed your hedgehog a variety of foods. This helps it get all the nutrients it needs. It also allows the animal to experience different textures. You can feed your hedgehog fruit, but only small amounts. Too much fruit can lead to health problems, such as **obesity**, **diabetes**, and dental disease.

ALL LATHERED UP

Hedgehogs have a peculiar behavior called "self-anointing." When hedgehogs encounter a new substance, they will chew it and form a lather with their saliva. Then they coat their spines with the lather. It is not known why hedgehogs anoint themselves. Some experts believe it is another form of protection from predators.

---

obesity—to be extremely overweight
diabetes—a disease in which there is too much sugar in the blood

BATHING AND GROOMING

Hedgehogs mostly groom themselves. You will only need to bathe your hedgehog about once a month. A bath will loosen bedding and dirt from their spines. Bathing your hedgehog more often can cause dry skin. Hedgehogs have toenails that need to be trimmed regularly. Clip the nails with small nail clippers. Be careful not to cut too deeply. It is easy to clip down into the soft part of the nail and cause bleeding.

A veterinarian can show you how to trim your pet's nails.

Learning how to properly hold a hedgehog will keep both you and your pet safe.

HEDGEHOG CONNECTION

Interacting daily with your hedgehog is a great way to create a strong connection. Start by taking your hedgehog out of its cage each day until it gets used to you. You do not need to wear gloves when you pick up a hedgehog. Its spines look dangerous, but they only give a slight prick. Pick your pet up by its sides. At first, it will probably be nervous and stay balled up. Gently rock it from side to side and rub its neck to get it to unroll.

Once you and your family are comfortable handling the hedgehog, take it out regularly. Play with it, give it treats, or just hold it. Another way to connect with your hedgehog is to talk to it so it learns to recognize your voice. Your hedgehog will also get to know your smell, especially if you hold it often. Make sure your family members also hold your hedgehog frequently.

CHAPTER 4

FUN AND GAMES

In many ways hedgehogs are just like you. They like to play, explore, and enjoy a treat now and then. Experiment with different ways to keep your hedgehog active, healthy, and stimulated.

A HEALTHY, HAPPY HEDGEHOG

Have you and your new hedgehog adjusted to one another? That's great! Now be sure to keep your pet happy and heathy. One way is to make sure your hedgehog's cage stays safe and fun. A large exercise wheel is key to making sure your hedgehog gets enough exercise. Hedgehogs often climb and explore. Set up a few levels of ramps and tunnels to keep your pet active. Try putting toilet paper tubes, PVC pipes, and small pieces of soft fabric in the cage. Your hedgehog can use its **foraging** and **rooting** skills if you scatter treats around for them to find.

forage—to search for food
root—to dig in the ground with the snout

Interacting with your hedgehog every day is an important way to bond with your pet.

HEDGEHOG ROUTINE

Although hedgehogs sleep during the day, your pet can adjust somewhat to your schedule. Late afternoons and evenings are good times to interact with your hedgehog. It will be more alert and active during this time. Sometimes hedgehogs are grouchy when they first wake up. They might also be grumpy when they are losing their baby spines during the quilling process. You will know when your pet is angry—it will make a clicking sound. The best thing to do when your pet is unhappy is to leave it alone. Try interacting with it again when it has calmed down. As you get to know and bond with your pet, you will learn its likes and dislikes.

Hedgehogs like to play with small boxes and paper bags.

TOYS AND TREATS

Giving your hedgehog toys to play with will help keep it healthy and active. You can make or buy all kinds of fun toys for your pet. Toys for cats and birds work well for hedgehogs. Hedgehogs will explore inside paper bags, oatmeal containers, and shoe boxes. Balls, bells, and chew toys also keep hedgehogs engaged.

Another fun way to interact with your pet is to give it treats. Insects or worms from a pet store make great treats. Some hedgehogs even eat scrambled eggs. Just do not give your pet too many treats—you do not want to spoil its appetite. Stay away from foods that are sugary, sticky, or salty.

ROOM TO RUN

Consider getting a pet playpen for your hedgehog. Your pet can run in this large area instead of just in its cage. Be careful if you bring your hedgehog outside. You do not want it to run away or be harmed by other animals. Keep it in an enclosed area where it is protected from harm and where you can keep an eye on it. If you let your hedgehog roam around in the grass, be sure the grass is free from harmful chemicals.

A MEMBER OF THE FAMILY

Each hedgehog has its own special personality. Some are very active. Others are quiet. Some like to be held while others like to be left alone. No matter the personality of your hedgehog, it can form a strong bond with you and become a beloved member of your family.

Spending time with your pet is the best way to form a lasting bond.

ROCKY MOUNTAIN HEDGEHOGS

The Rocky Mountain Hedgehog Show is held every year in Colorado. The weekend-long show has guest speakers, vendors, and fun competitions, all related to hedgehogs. The competitions include a race in which hedgehogs jump over tiny hurdles just 0.5 inch (1.3 cm) off the ground!

Take the time to learn all about hedgehogs not only before you adopt one, but after it has joined your home. Read books and have a parent help you research online. Consider joining a hedgehog club as well. Here you can get to know other hedgehog owners and share tips and stories. Look for a hedgehog show in your area. The more you know about these cute animals, the better you can care for one. Pet hedgehogs typically live for 8 to 10 years. By taking good care of your hedgehog, you can enjoy many years together.

GLOSSARY

adapt (uh-DAPT)—to change to fit into a new or different situation

breeder (BREE-der)—a person who raises animals to sell

diabetes (dy-uh-BEE-teez)—a disease in which there is too much sugar in the blood

environment (in-VY-ruhn-muhnt)—the surroundings in which a person, animal, or plant lives

forage (FOR-ij)—to search for food

mammal (MAM-uhl)—a warm-blooded animal that breathes air; mammals have hair or fur; female mammals feed milk to their young

native (NAY-tuhv)—growing or living naturally in a particular place

nocturnal (nok-TUR-nuhl)—active at night and resting during the day

obesity (oh-BEE-sih-tee)—to be extremely overweight

omnivore (OM-nuh-vor)—an animal that eats both plants and other animals

predator (PRED-uh-tur)—an animal that hunts other animals for food

root (ROOT)—to dig in the ground with the snout

solitary (SOL-uh-ter-ee)—living and hunting alone

species (SPEE-sheez)—a group of animals with common features

temperament (TEM-pur-uh-muhnt)—the combination of an animal's behavior and personality; the way an animal usually acts or responds to situations shows its temperament

READ MORE

Fortescue, Madeleine. *Super Skin: Spines, Quills, and Plates.* Ultimate Animal Defenses. New York: Gareth Stevens Publishing, 2017.

Gregory, Josh. *Hedgehogs.* Nature's Children. New York: Childrens Press, 2016.

Mattern, Joanne. *Porcupines and Hedgehogs.* Animal Look-Alikes. Egremont, Mass.: Red Chair Press, 2017.

Matzke, Ann. *Hedgehog.* You Have a Pet What?!. Vero Beach, Fla.: Rourke Educational Media, 2015.

INTERNET SITES

Use FactHound to find Internet sites related to this book.

Visit *www.facthound.com*

Just type in 9781543530568 and go.

INDEX